1

I slowly stumble down the pavement, my head held low. Cold air wafting around, as I breathe mist comes out my mouth, twirls and then vanishes into thin air. All I can hear is the beep of vans as they drive past and various newspaper sellers yelling:

"Snow Tonight!"

"Wrap Up Warm!"

"Drive Safely!"

I look up and my heart rises! We have not had snow here in the small town of Subbstring since 1915 and it is now 1981. I fiddle around in my pockets for any spare lunch money from school. I take out a two-pound coin and a fifty pence piece; I have just enough for a sledge!

I wait for a car to go past and then run across the road as fast as I can to the DIY shop. It is an old building and a bit dodgy but it always has what I need. I walk up to it and the fresh winter air fills my nose.

"Forecast says a foot of snow!" says another newspaper seller as a man runs past him in a posh outfit. The newspaper seller looks at me. "I'd get home quickly kiddo before it comes!"

I nod at him and continue running till I get to an old rickety wooden building with a sign saying DIY that is about to fall off. There are a few crates outside filled with coal and logs that I walk past to get to the door. I push it open slowly and a small bell chimes.

I look around and turn to the counter. No ones there.

"Hello?" I call.

There is a long pause then a sudden creek as a huge, mountain of a man walks through a door that I did not even notice was there. He had a log over his shoulder and a long mousy beard. Fear floods through me, the nice man who used to work here must have quit! The huge bulky figure dropped the log with a grunt and a crash which made the whole room shake. He slowly struts towards me as I back for the door but miss and instead fall onto the wall next to it. There is silence.

"What you doin' here kid."

I smile. This isn't a scary beast, it's Hax!

Hax was a lumberjack who helped me find my way home the first time I had to walk back from school. He was so nice it seemed like he had met me before but I know he had not. I was eight then, now I'm twelve so I wonder if he recognises me.

"Hax!" I say and hug him.

"Rocco?" he says, "Rocco is that you?"

"Yep," I say stepping back and grinning at him.

"What are you here for?" He says as he walks behind the counter.

"Oh, a sledge please!" I say excitedly, "for the snow!"

"There ain't gonna be no snow tonight," came a croaky voice.

An old lady came staggering from one of the isles.

"There hasn't been snow in Subbstring in sixty-six years, you think it is just gonna blow over tonight!" she croaks, waving her arms about.

"I dunno Mrs Turnip the forecast does say that there is going to be a foot of it blowing over from the east," says Hax with a roll of his eyes.

"Don't you trust that Fork-ask," She yells waving her snake-skin walking-stick at him, "It's witch craft it is!"

I let out I small giggle.

"And you boy," she turns to me "You're the one that lives with your Gran in the house next to me."

I nod.

"Step on my lawn once more and YOU WON'T HAVE FEET TO STEP ON IT WITH!" she stumbles out the door mumbling "children! They are a work of witch craft!"

I turn to Hax and let out all my laughter. He smiles too.

"Anyway," he says "sledges are three pounds."

"Oh," I look at the money in my hand, "I only have two pounds fifty."

"You can have it," he says with a wink.

I smile.

"Thanks!"

2

I happily run up the path to my Grandma's house, my new red sledge sliding at my feet. The house is white with ivy crawling up the walls. I ring the door bell and my Grandma opens it with a smile.

"How was your day Rocco?" she says with a grin.

"Great!" I say, "Did you know Hax now runs the DIY shop!"

She looks at my sledge and smiles.

"Isn't that wonderful dear!" she says.

"It's for the snow!" I jump up in glee.

"I heard about the snow," she says "we might finally have a snow day tomorrow. Now come inside, it's time for dinner."

I hop in and she closes the door behind me. I have been living with my Grandma since I was two and a bit. I do not remember much of my parents, there was a loud noise, then a scream, I was upside down, there were sirens, blue and red flashes, and then I was being held by something big, feeling it's cold breath on my small head. But that's all. I have never been able to work it out and my Grandma will only tell me it was a car crash, how vague is that!

Anyway, I sit on my chair next to the fire place and watch Newsround while my Grandma slowly knits in the corner.

"Snow is coming in from the East!" says the man on the news, his name is apparently Dr Flibbertigibbet, but I'm not so sure how correct that is, "Snuggle up warm tonight we are going to have the white January of a life time!"

I grab the remote and pause the tv.

"Grandma, do you need your medicine yet?" I say.

She looks at me and stops knitting.

"Oh yes dear, do you want me to," she begins to slowly get up when I interrupt her:

"No Gran I'll get them."

"Oh, thanks dear."

I slowly walk out the room and towards the kitchen, I can't get the thought of snow out my head! I have never seen snow, I wonder what it is like; is it fluffy and soft, or is it hard like ice?

I open the cabinet above the stove and see that we have three pills left, which is perfect; one for tonight, one for tomorrow morning and one for tomorrow afternoon. It's also good because we definitely won't be able to get to the shops if there is snow. I grab a pill and look out the window just before I leave. There is no snow yet but maybe it will start coming later.

I slowly walk back into the living room and give my grandma the pill.

"Thank you, Rocco," she says.

I sit down and watch her, she is about seventy-five, her hair is messy and white with a purple tint and she always wears an ugly Christmas jumper even if it is January. To keep the fun going, I think. She has big round eyes that are emerald green and she always wears purple lipstick.

"It's not snowing yet," she says suddenly, looking out the window.

"Maybe it will start later tonight," I say.

"Hopefully," she says with a grin, "now it's off to bed for you! You need to be well rested to play in the snow if there is any."

"Ok Grandma," I say and I dash out the room and up the stairs.

<u>3</u>

I slowly open my eyes, tired. It is Thursday morning and my alarm clock keeps screaming. I sit up in bed, blink and my eyes crunch a little before I walk into my bathroom and look in the mirror. My face is droopy and I have a severe case of bed hair, each brown strand facing in opposite directions. I brush my hair, clean my teeth and get out of my pyjamas and into some clothes when I remember: how did I forget!

I run to my window and pull the blinds open...

Snow! Tons of it, endless drapes of white sheets covering the ground, sprinkled in the trees and covering all the plants and bushes!

"SNOW!" I yell as I run downstairs into my Grandma's room, "SNOW!"

I turn on the lights and start jumping on her bed.

"GRANDMA! SNOW!"

"Ugh, what is it Rocco," she says getting up and reaching for her spectacles.

"SNOW!" I say again, feeling excitement like no other.

She looks out the window and smiles.

"How lovely!" she says.

I hug her and sprint out the room. I keep running until I get to the front door.

"SNOW!" I yell as I burst through collapsing onto the soft white powder.

I laugh. It is so cool! It was definitely worth the wait! I lay on my back in the snow and watch the cream clouds float in the sky.

"Rocco."

My Grandma opens the door, squinting.

"Rocco, I think I dropped my spectacles in the snow, would you mind."

I get up, run to her and sigh.

"They are in your pocket Gran," I say taking a pair of cotton candy coloured glasses out of her dressing gown.

"Oh, sorry dear," she says while she rubs the lenses with her finger.

"Would you like me to get your pills for you," I say with a giggle.

"Oh, yes please, I'm not feeling so well."

I walk past her and back into the house. I cannot get over the thought of how cool snow is! I get to the kitchen, open the cupboard and my heart stops.

No way! How could a perfectly good day go so wrong in a second! One, only one. Wiry, grey fur, beady eyes and a long damp tale.

I scream and the rat scurries away back down its hole in the back of the cupboard. After a few seconds pass I bite my lip and walk back to see the damage; the rat had eaten the last of Grandma's pills!

"No!" I say under my breath.

What do I do now! Grandma needs those pills to stop her getting ill!

"Grandma," I say gravely, slowly walking back towards the doorway.

"What is it dear?" she says turning to me.

"A rat ate your pills," I say not knowing what else to do, "it must have scurried inside to take shelter from the snow last night!"

"Oh no!" she says "It's Ok Rocco, I can go a day without them."

She coughs and sits on a chair and I can tell she is not well already.

"No Grandma," I say, "I'll sledge down the road and go to the pharmacy."

"The pharmacy will be closed!" she says, "you just enjoy the snow."

She coughs again.

"No, it'll only take ten minutes, trust me!" I say and I walk out the room.

4

I get my sledge out the garage and stand outside my house, the cold air swiping at my face. I stare at the neighbourhood. It looks so pretty in the snow, shimmering white everywhere. I have two options, I sledge through the dark forest where I was told to never go, or I can take the route that goes right down the street. The most obvious option is the road, I cannot risk the forest.

How does this work? I begin to think. I have never used a sledge before, only seen them from the photos of my cousins in America. I put my sledge down on the floor and before I get on it, I turn back to face my house.

"I will be back soon Grandma," I promise myself.

I turn back around. What? Where is it? I look around and my heart stops. The sledge is sliding down the hill, but not to the street, right across to Mrs Turnips house!

"No!" I yell at it as if it would listen.

I run after it, flicking snow up in my view. I keep sprinting. I cannot believe this happened! And it could have been any garden but it had to be Mrs Turnip's. I keep running until I see the sledge turn around the corner of her house and out of view! I gasp and run quicker.

I skid round the side of the house, snow spraying at my feet, then stop and look around. My heart sinks. The sledge is a few meters away with mud trail behind it and about ten flattened flowers lie in the ruined dirt.

I look up at the window. Mrs Turnip does not seem to be home. I slowly tiptoe towards the sledge. I cannot believe this happened, but I'm just going to grab the sledge and run. I reach it, look around again, just in case anyone noticed, then pick it up.

I carefully walk around the other side of the house.

"YOU!"

I jump and scream. Mrs Turnip is standing an inch away from me, her outstretched finger nearly touching my nose.

"I told you not to come here again!" She snaps.

Suddenly she raises her arm, gripping tight onto a rake. My heart races! I quickly put my sledge down and jump on it just in time for her to smack the rake down into the snow where I was once standing. She looks around puzzled at how I disappeared, only to look behind her and see me gliding swiftly down to the road.

"NO!" I hear her yell and I look back; she's chasing me! That crazy woman!

I speed up. This is fun! I glide down the bank and turn onto the road. Then I hear loud crunching footsteps and turn around. She is getting closer! I speed up by leaning forwards. It feels like I'm flying, on the ground that is, and with some mad woman chasing me.

I had no idea she could run so fast! I'm sure she's like eighty! I guess if something pushes her over the edge that much, she'll go for it!

I can't help but look back at her as she runs after me, her rake uplifted.

"WOAH!" I scream! I hadn't been paying attention! I was heading for a big curved bump in the snow!

I panic and try to turn away, but I can't make it in time! What should I do! But before I could do anything my sledge rides up the slope and takes off backwards!

"AGH!" I holler as I fly over Mrs Turnip as she looks up in awe at me and I flip around to crash onto something hard, then black-out.

5

I wake up to thousands of burning cold snowflakes whipping onto me. I open my eyes. Everything is blurry. It is snowing harder than ever. I feel like I'm moving. I try to stand up but instantly fall over.

"Yep," I say to myself lying on snow, "I'm moving."

I look around the sky is grey, full of clouds and all that surrounds me are snowy fields that zoom past. Then it hits me! I'm high up and moving, I must be on a van! I look over the edge, scared. Hang on, this is not a van, it's a gritting lorry!

What do I do! How far has this gritting lorry taken me from home. I slowly turn around on my front, petrified that I'll fall over.

Suddenly there is a loud screech and the gritting lorry comes to a sharp halt. I'm flicked over, snow in my eyes as I fall off the edge and slide down the front windscreen with a scream.

I hear a door open and someone walks out.

"Agh! Warwick, the tyres are stuck in the snow!" Comes a husky voice.

"Well to be fair," says a more muffled and squeaky voice from inside the lorry, "It is snowing heavily."

It's true, the more I lie here the more I can feel the cold snow and air slicing through me. I decide to ask for help and slowly get up, push myself off the bonnet and walk around the side.

"Excuse me," I say.

A man who is looking under the lorry near the tyre jumps and looks at me.

"What are you doing here kid!"

"Well..."

"Who are you!"

He stares at me. He has short grey hair and a curly moustache that has caught all the snowflakes that fell upon it. He is wearing a big fur coat with a fluffy hood.

"Sorry," I say, "I'm Rocco, from Subbstring."

"SUBBSTRING!" He says in shock, "We must have past there hours ago!"

My mouth drops!

"Hours ago! No! This can't be happening! I need to get back! My Grandma! The pills!"

"Come inside 'Rocco'," He says nodding his head to the door.

I jump in shivering. The lorry warms me up as I sit in the middle seat. I look at the windscreen. How did they not notice me fall down it, there is a big child shaped slide mark!

"Basset just get in the car," comes the squeaky voice, "Oh!"

I turn around to see a short but plump man in the driving seat. He has a blonde fringe, but the top of his head is covered by a blue bobble hat, for some reason he reminds me a bit of humpty dumpty.

"Hello?" He says slowly.

"Sorry," I reply, "Your friend invited me in, I'm Rocco."

"Well," He squeaks wearily, "Hi Rocco, I'm Warwick and this is my friend Basset."

I turn around to see the man with a moustache getting into the car and pulling down his snowy hood. Basset is much taller and bulkier than Warwick making them quite a weird match.

"So kid," says Basset, "You said you are from Subbstring?"

"Yeah," I reply, "My neighbour was chasing me while I was on my sledge and…"

My sledge! It must have fallen off the lorry but I hope it is still in one piece!

"…I hit a piece of snow," I continue, "Which sent me flying and think I must have landed on your lorry."

"That must have been when we were gritting the roads in Subbstring," says Basset.

"And I'm sure I fainted," I finish.

"Subbstring was at least an hour ago," Warwick squeaks.

"Unfortunately, there is no turning back in this weather," Basset says.

I look out the side window and see snow hammering down.

I sigh.

"What's wrong kid?" asks Basset slowly.

"I was getting pills for my Grandma, without them she will be very sick, she could even die!" I close my eyes to think and pause, "I have to get back!"

"Sorry but unless the snow clears that can't happen," says Warwick.

"Then I have to walk!" I say opening my eyes again.

"No!" Basset stares at me, "We can't let an eight-year-old run around in this weather alone!"

"First of all, I'm twelve," I begin to climb over Basset towards the door, "and I have no choice!"

Basset says nothing but pushes me back.

"I'm sorry Rocco," Warwick squeaks.

There is a long pause while I realise that there is nothing I can do. I can't believe it. My grandma!

Basset opens a can of beer and sits back drinking. That's when I have an idea.

"Do you like beer Basset?" I ask him.

"Agh I love it kid," He says whipping the froth off his moustache, "I could drink ten cans in a minute!"

I look at Warwick and he nods.

"I bet you can't!"

Basset lowers his can and stares at me in dismay. I knew it, I knew he would be competitive.

"Is that a challenge," He grunts at me.

I smile.

"Tell you what kid, I could do TWENTY!"

I tilt my head to the stack of beer cans below his seat. He laughs at me.

"Count," He says picking them up.

"Ready… Steady… Go!"

He starts chugging the first one and it's not long till he's on the third. I smile, my plan is working! It is actually working!

By the eighth one his eyes are all ready starting to float to the back of his head.

"You don't look so good," squeaks Warwick in disgust.

"Shut up!" Basset coughs with a mouthful of beer and froth.

It is bizarre really, he kind of starts to go green.

"Ew," Warwick gags as he starts to open the door, "I'll go get you a paper bag so that you don't vomit in my lorry!"

Warwick walks out the lorry door and I hear the back open. By the time I turn back to Basset he is looking like a zombie!

"I'm sure I put the bags in the back here," Comes Warwick's voice as he rummages around back there.

Basset is on about his eleventh and… he crashes into the footwell of the lorry.

<u>6</u>

I stare at him. My plan actually worked!

"Is this the bag, nope that's a sock," I hear Warwick say as he rummages around in the back.

I open the glove compartment and there are some post-it notes and a pen.

To Warwick and Basset

Thank you for letting me rest in your lorry for a bit and I'm sorry to leave like this but I have to get back to Subbstring to get my Grandma's pills. I hope you understand.

-Rocco

I stick it on the dashboard and climb over Basset who is still slumped in the footwell. I open the door trying to be as quiet as possible and once it is open, I step out and run for it, the snow crunching under my feet. I get off the road and make it up the bank to the trees when I turn back the way the lorry came.

Warwick still has not noticed, he is still rummaging in the back of the lorry.

"Hang on, is this a sock?" I hear him say before I rush into the woods.

The leaves block the snow from falling down however it's still freezing. I try not to think about it, but I have to get back to Subbstring. The forest is usually dark and creepy but the snow lights it up. I walk on, my legs already aching.

I think about my Grandma. Is she Ok? Basset said Subbstring was an hour away so I've been gone for at least one and a half when I said I would be only ten minutes. I hope she's not worried, or sick, I need to get these pills quickly!

Only now do I realise that I'm lost. I look around, every tree looks the same! How do I know I'm even heading toward Subbstring, I could be going in the opposite direction. I wipe the snow off a fallen log and sit down for a second. I let out a sigh and the mist comes out my mouth again.

I rest my head on the tree behind and try to close my eyes. I'm tired, really tired.

There's a sudden crackle of dead leaves and I bolt upright, my eyes scanning the area. It sounds like an animal. There it is again, another crackle sound from behind a bush.

I slowly get up and creep towards it. What is it! I'm scared. Before I get to the bush a cloud white paw becomes visible. I jump back, my heart racing. The creature slowly moves further out. I close my eyes in fear, say it's not...

I hover, one eye open, I can see it. A wolf! It's messy grey and white fur, a body about a meter long, with a tail that falls onto the snow and piercing red eyes!

I scream and instantly start running, the sound of its feet chasing after me. I look over my shoulder at it but as I do, I trip over a tree root. It slows down and is just a foot away from me. I hope it can't see me because there is a small dip that I'm lying in. Aching all over, I can hear the sound of its nose twitching but there was a worse sound that came of it just then. A howl. A loud one. That echoed throughout the whole woods.

I sit up and become much more frightened; about five more wolves appear near my left, four near my right and about three join the main one behind me.

I'm breathing heavily and loudly. I can't help it, I'm petrified. I decide to slowly walk forward, not looking back. I'm on my tiptoes, my face screwed up.

SNAP!
My eyes travel down to the stick beneath my feet. I look back at the fourteen wolves all glaring at me.

I run for my life, screaming and listening to the pounding of paws and the howling of the pack.

"HELP!" I yell as I dodge the trees and sprint through the snowy woods, "HELP!"

A stitch grows in my side and I can hear them getting closer, but I don't stop, sheer panic keeps me going. The wolves howl again. This isn't happening, tell me this isn't happening!

I look to my side and notice there is two right next to me! They are trying to trap me in! I speed up. Please don't eat me please!

7

I keep running. The wolves gaining on me and closing in.

"WOAH!" I trip over my own legs and just lie on my front in the snow.

I shut my eyes, this is how I die? I hear them slowly creeping in on me. I hope my Grandma gets her pills, maybe Warwick and Basset will get them for her, although I doubt it after how I left. Ugh, why did I have to do that, I was so safe in there, and a lorry is much quicker. What was I thinking!

I feel a wolf's nose sniff up my leg and to my back. Its warm breath penetrating through my clothes…

"HEY! HEY! SCATTER!"

I hear the whimper of all the wolves as they spin around and scurry off in the opposite direction. I slowly open my eyes to see a large figure standing next to me with a long beard.

"HAX!" I yell in glee and I instantly fling my arms around him, "Hax, thank you, thank you so much."

I begin crying as I lay my head on his warm chest.

"Shhh," He says hugging me, "Rocco you're safe now, you're safe."

I let go of him and slowly calm down.

"Hax, there was one and then fourteen and then!"

"You're Ok," He smiles through his ginger beard.

I let out a deep breath and feel relaxed again. But only now is it that I notice a big cow, standing next to Hax, pulling along a little wooden waggon. It is white covered in brown splodges like paint. I try to look at its face but it is far too interested in a little snow drop flower surrounded by moss.

"Hax."

"Yes Rocco," He looks at me.

"Who's the cow?" I ask.

Hax looks at it.

"This is Tori, say hi Tori, TORI!" Hax steps on the rein and the cow swings around to face me.

She has a sort of flat face with big blue eyes and a rounded pink nose. One of her ears has a yellow tag on and she wears a big bell around her neck. She tilts her head and stares at me.

"Um, hi Tori," I say waving.

Tori jumps and her bell jingles.

I'm so relieved Hax showed up, I was so close to death. Then it hits me, what are the odds that he was in the same forest as me, miles away, when I was in danger.

"Hax?"

"Yes Rocco."

I look from Tori to Hax.

"Why are you here, I mean how did you know I was here."

"Well first of all, I could hear you scream for help from a mile away," We smile at each other and he continues, "but also, after you were gone for a while, your Grandma called the police…"

My mouth drops. My Grandma got that worried. No! That wasn't what I wanted to happen.

"… I saw the police at your house and went to go look for you," Hax finished.

"Oh," I say and look at the ground, "My grandma's not worried, is she?"

"No," Hax grins at me, "I told her I'd find you and she was very relaxed."

I let out a sigh of relief.

"But what about the pills! Was she coughing at all when you talked to her!"

"Rocco, don't worry," Hax puts a hand on my shoulder, "we just need to get you home."

Tori scoops her head under me, lifting me onto her back. She takes me to a small, moss covered waggon. I climb in.

"Thanks Tori," I say as I pat her on the head.

She rings her bell again and trots around to the front. Hax follows and ties Tori back onto the cart. We start moving, Tori pulling it along.

Then it hits me, Hax is taking me home.

"No! I can't go home! I need to get my Grandma's pills," I shout to him.

Hax turns around to face me.

"Rocco, you have been away for long enough, look how much danger you were in," He says, "I must take you home!"

"But what if my Grandma gets badly ill without them!" I shout, "Who would be there to look after me, after my parents were in the car crash, she is the only family I have left!"

Hax shuts his eyes.

"I remember the night your parent's car crashed. Your Grandma promised to look after you no matter what!"

Hax looks off down the forest, "She can't lose you too."

"And I can't lose her!" I argue back.

"She is Ok."

"But what if she isn't!" I pause, "and anyway why can't anyone tell me what happened that night I lost my parents!"

"Because we don't know!" Hax stares at me sadly which takes me by surprise, I have only ever seen him cheery.

"You don't," I say looking at the bottom of the waggon.

"Rocco, no one does."

8

It's getting dark, a day has gone by already! No! I need to get to the pharmacy, my Grandma needs those pills, she's already gone a day without them!

"Oh, c'mon Tori!" Hax shouts, it's not fair on the poor cow, you can tell she is tired because she's slowing down, a lot.

But Hax shouldn't be yelling at her, we're all tired and we've all had a long day.

"Hax," I say, trying to calm him down, "It's late, Tori is probably just as tired as we are." The cow moos as if agreeing with me. "Maybe we just need to stop somewhere for the night."

Tori stops pulling the wagon and Hax slowly turns to face me.

"You're right Rocco," He shuts his eyes, takes a deep breath and then looks at me again, "but where will we sleep, its freezing and we are in the middle of the woods!"

He's right, everything is covered head to foot in a white glaze of snow, if we do fall asleep, we'll most likely get hypothermia! I sigh, what are we going to do!

Suddenly, the roar of a motorbike echoes from the distance. I look up at Hax, he's smiling from ear to ear.

"Hax, what was…" I'm cut off by his excitement.

"Rocco! I know where we are! There is a bed and breakfast pub right through these trees!" he looks ahead and points to a small light shining through the snowy leaves, "We can spend the night there!"

My heart rises, yes!

We leave the wagon there, stumble through the trees and onto a small road. My heart sinks back down.

"Um… Hax?"

Hax looks at me and sighs.

"Ok, I know it doesn't look very…"

"KID FRIENDLY!" I yell!

This is definitely not a normal bed and breakfast, it is an old bikers pub with a few rooms on top. Motorcycles chained to some stands, weird smoke coming from one window, and a sign saying;

Welkum too yee old bed and brekfast pub!

"It'll be fine," says Hax as a scream can be heard from an open window.

Umm… I'm scared, there is no other way to put it. It looks like I could get murdered in a second in this place! Ugh, but I guess it's the best place to stay over. I look at Tori, I think she is as worried as I am.

The three of us cross the snowy road and onto the other pavement.

"I'm gonna have to leave you here Tori," Hax says as he ties a rope from Tori's bell to a small sign post saying;

𝒩oe 𝒦idz aloud

I read it and my eyes widen, but I won't mention it, it'll make things worse. I look up at a window with a small light coming from it, what if every room is full? I look behind me as two people race past on a motorbike laughing.

"C'mon then!"

I spin around and Hax is holding the old oak door for me.

"Ok," I say as I slowly and wearily step past him into the pub.

My shoes crunch on the floor due to it being covered in sawdust. It's much warmer in here, out of the snow and I can smell whiskey and tobacco. It's weird, everyone in here seems to be huge, rounded men with wiry beards, in fact, I don't think there is even one female here.

The door closes behind me and Hax joins by my side. There is a small fire place in the corner, tables and benches scattered about, very few windows and a small bar in the opposite corner to the fire place.

"Why don't you take a seat while I go talk to the bar tender about booking a room," Hax says roughly.

"Wait, no Hax don't leave me alone here!" I panic, chasing after him.

I know he says to trust this place but I don't like the feel of it. He stops and turns to face me.

"I'll make sure no one hurts you," he says with a small laugh, pointing to a table near another door labelled; BED ROMES.

I sigh.

"Fine."

I feel like everyone's looking at me, I know they are not because of the loud sound of laughter and booing at the tv. Hax has already gone towards the bar, I may as well just take a seat.

Nervously, I amble towards the bench, brush some dust off, and sit down. I'm quite close to the fire which is heating me up nicely. It's better being in the corner of the room I guess, because no one can really see you.

Hax is talking to the bar tender who is probably the largest man here, oh, I take that back, it's a woman.

My eyes are drawn to the poorly laminated menu on the table.

DRINKS;

- **BRITISH BEER**
- **IRISH BEER**
- **SCOTTISH BEER**
- **LESS-BRITISH BEER**

"Basset would love this place," I laugh to myself.

I stop, it's only then I hear the sound of boots crunching in the sawdust as they move towards me. I look up. Petrified. A huge brawny bloke is making his way towards me. He takes his incredibly thick arm and wipes some drops of beer off his wild beard before he sits down opposite me. My heart is racing but I keep calm as he slowly tilts his head and stares at me. There is a long awkward silence which is suddenly ruined by his low growling voice;

"Cain?"

I jump up and his greyish brown eyes follow me. Did he really just call me...

"Hey guys," he says, beckoning some other bikers over, "It's mini Cain!"

My heart races as they all leave the pool table and strut towards me.

"I'm just gonna go," I slowly mumble.

"No, no," Says a huge bald guy from beside me.

I spin around, horrified. They are all surrounding me, all the bulky, scary ruffians.

"HAX!" I holler, begging for help even though I can no longer see him.

"'e looks just like 'is father dun'e? Sledge 'ammer."

Oh, what a nice nickname, I think, mortified. A big thug slowly nods, getting closer till I can't see anything apart from huge stomachs.

"Look," I say, trying to stay calm, "I don't know who you are, so can I just get on with my day, and *not* get to know you."

I slowly back away but one grabs me by the scruff of my shirt.

"So soon, we wan'ed to get to know ya."

He starts lifting me up till I can no longer feel the ground. I hear them all laughing in their deep, grumbly voices.

"Please let me go!"

"Wha' ya gonna do otherwise?!"

Right, that's it. I lift my foot and deliver a hard kick to his shin. The biker immediately drops me to the floor and falls back onto the table, causing it to snap in half due to his weight.

There is a pause as the rest of the thugs stare at me. Uh oh...

9

I make a run for the other side of the room, the group of bikers chasing me.

"GET THAT KID!" one shouts.

Thinking quickly, I try to jump onto the pool table but one of the bikers grabs my ankle. I reach out, grab the eight ball and chuck it at him. It hits him in the forehead and he lets go, clutching his hands round his face.

I scramble up and stand on the table, petrified. My heart is pounding as another brute jumps onto the other end, this one is a woman, yet she has a thicker neck than some of the men.

"C'mon then kid!" she yells with a toothy grin.

She swings a punch at me but I duck under, running behind her.

"UGH!"

Her breathing is like an animal, her chest rising higher than her chin with every intake. She begins to run towards me but I pick up the cue and swing it onto her shins, causing her to double over and fall off the table and take out two other bikers.

I jump off the table and sprint towards the bar. Hax isn't there, where is he?!

I turn around just in time to see a beer bottle fly towards me. I quickly duck and it smashes onto the wall, glass flying all over the room.

I look back up, shaking. There are three more huge guys glaring at me. I make eye contact with one and his lips twitch.

"I'm not normally a violent person you know," says the man who came up to me first.

I let out a small unintended laugh.

"You think that's funny, do you?" He growls, chucking another beer bottle at me.

I jump out the way and it smashes through one of the only windows, setting off a car alarm. Oh my god, I think, this can't be happening right now.

I slowly get up just as one rugby tackles me and sends me flying over the bar table and crashing onto the floor on the other side.

"Ouch," I moan, feeling like my back just snapped in half.

I stand up again and brush the straw off my t-shirt.

"Quick question," I ask, "how did you know my father?"

The man chucks another bottle at me and I take refuge behind the bar, allowing it to smash into a cabinet with glasses.

"Let's just say he was a friend from work," he replies when I jump up again.

Without giving me time to think they all charge at me. I panic and grab the lemonade dispenser hose and spray it everywhere, the sheer force sends the hooligans flying to the wall.

"ROCCO?"

"STOP STOP!"

I turn around to see Hax and the bartender in the doorway, not realising that I'm still holding the hose! The two of them fall to the ground, completely covered in lemonade.

"TURN IT OFF!" the bartender yells!

I quickly drop it and it turns off. There is a long pause and I realise how manic that was. There is a huge man lying in the remains of the bench, the woman completely flattening two bikers, three of the other thugs, Hax and the bartender completely covered in lemonade and glass everywhere.

Hax runs and hugs me.

"Hax!" I say, "I'm so sorry!"

"Don't worry Rocco it's not your fault it's theirs."

Hax turns to the bartender and shrugs.

"So... about that room..."

The bartender, surrounded by about twelve angry ruffians stares at us.

"Get out," the bartender says bristling.

We both turn around and walk out the door, back into the cold winter street. It's snowing and Tori is pressed up against the wall, almost petrified of every little white snowflake.

"C'mon Tori," says Hax, untying her from the sign post.

"I'm sorry Hax," I say as the snow falls onto me from the night sky," The bikers just started to attack me and..."

Hax turns around and laughs.

"Rocco, it's not your fault! I should have known they wouldn't take you nicely in there. I'm just glad you are safe now."

I smile and we cross the street, back into the shelter of the woods.

"But I completely wrecked that guys pub!" I say, the leaves cracking beneath our feet as we walk towards Hax's wagon.

"So," Hax says, "I nicked some bedding!"

He takes some blankets out of his shirt. I stare at him, jaw dropped but slightly laughing.

"But... what... why?!"

"I knew they weren't gonna let a child in so I asked to see one of the rooms and when he wasn't looking, I just slipped it under my shirt," He smiles and winks at me.

I laugh out loud in the snowy woodlands.

<u>10</u>

I slip under a blanket, Hax has made us two tent like structures with the bedding and some logs.

I lie on my stomach, my head propped under my forearms. I'm opposite Hax and between us is a small crackling bonfire I made while he was sorting the small tents out.

It's very peaceful really, just sleeping outside in the snow, the stars twinkling through gaps in the orange leaves. But then I remember what one of the bikers said back at the pub.

"Hax?" I ask.

"Yes Rocco."

"One of the guys who attacked me back at the pub said he new my dad, and it was from 'work'."

Hax closes his eyes and sighs.

"Rocco I just can't tell you, it's not the right time."

I slightly laugh out of spite.

"Hax, I was just attacked by twelve angry hooligans, all of who knew my father, if I'm not ready after that, I don't know when I will be!"

He looks up at me through the fire.

"Rocco, your parents Cain and Sasha were my best friends, we knew each other since secondary school. You recognised me the day I helped you get to school because I used to always see you as a baby," He brakes off, and starts breathing quickly, his eyes closed.

"C'mon Hax I'm ready to know!"

He looks at me and continues;

"I met your Dad at the beginning of year nine. I was new and he was the one who toured me around. Ever since then we were best friends, we would always hang out at breaks and even prank the teachers. Your Dad was a very clever man, he would always score incredibly high in exams.

One day when me and him were walking around town, he bumped into this girl in the supermarket. He instantly ran to me from another isle, telling me he had bumped into and instantly fell in love with this girl. I took him into the bathrooms where we stood him in front of the mirror and did his hair, tucked his shirt in, made him more presentable. Then we rushed out and saw a tall blond girl with baby blue eyes and glasses checking her stuff at the till, Cain was nervous at first but I pushed him up and they started talking, well if you call this talking;

"Hi."

"Hey."

"Hi."

"Hey."

"You wanna?"

"Go to the cinema?"

"Umm... Yeah."

"Yep."

"Yeah."

"Cool."

"Cool..."

Come to think of it, I don't remember if Sasha paid for her stuff. Anyway, your dad and your mum became really close. We all graduated together the three of us, and when your mother and father got married, I was the best man.

Then your Dad became an accountant and your Mum a doctor, my GCSE's weren't as high so I became a lumberjack. But we were always close friends. Then on June the 2nd 1969, they had you. It was the happiest day I can remember.

But things went down hill from there at your Dad's work, he was put in charge of firing people. Cain was such a nice and shy man, it just wasn't the job for him. But as he was forced to fire more people, he made more enemies. Once unemployed, the people he fired would go to that pub back there to moan about him.

Then, then in 1971 I got a phone call saying that... saying that," Hax broke off, choked with tears.

My heart felt like stone, I felt like hugging him and never letting go.

"Saying that there was a car cash," Hax continued "I instantly dropped the phone and ran to the small roadway where there was an over-turned car, ambulances and police cars surrounding it, and two white clothes on the road covering ..."

There's a long pause as I stare at him through the small crackling fire.

"I'll never forget the loud sirens, the flashes of blue and red. The first thing I did was get on my knees and crawl into the ruin of the car. The police men were yelling at me not to but I had to check if you were alright, I knew that was what they would want me to do. I reached over to the small two-year-old boy crying as he hung upside down in his booster seat. I unplugged his seat belt and held him tightly in my arms, coming out of the car slowly and carefully.

There was a little cut on your head but you were ok. I remember the policeman trying to tell me to give you over, but I didn't trust him, I didn't trust any of it. I ran through the woods. Sprinting with you crying in my arms. It was dark and gloomy, the wind was howling though the trees.

"Shhh, shhh," I was saying, trying to calm you down.

That was when I stopped, I heard a twig snap. I looked around.

"GO AWAY!" I boomed and whatever it was ran off.

Then, I took you to your grandma and promised to always be there for you if you needed."

I get out of the blankets as Hax buries his head in his pillow and run over to him, past Tori as she slept up against a tree and slipped into Hax's tent. I hug him.

"Rocco," says Hax, turning to face me, "Rocco, I don't know many things, but one thing I do know is, your parents car crash wasn't an accident, with all the enemies your father had unwillingly made, it doesn't add up."

My eyes widen as I stare at him.

"Who do you think..."

"I don't know, but back there at the pub, I recognised that man," He opens his eyes, "But don't worry about it, it can't be. Anyway, I think it time you got to bed."

I don't say any more, I just stumble back into my tent and try to sleep, but I can't help thinking of that guy's devil smile back at the pub, was he the one who caused my parents death?

"Oh, by the way, Rocco," I hear Hax's voice.

I sit up and look at him. He smiles.

"I'll help you get the pills for your Grandma."

<u>11</u>

I wake up early that morning to see Hax packing away his tent. It's early and there is almost double the amount of snow there was last night.

"MOOO!"

I jump as Tori runs towards me and suddenly licks my face. Yuck. I wipe the saliva off of me and consider it as a 'good morning lick.'

"Hax," I yawn, my feet aching in the shoes I slept in, "Did it snow that much over night?"

"Yep," He says, turning around after packing the sheets into the waggon, "on the bright side though I found a new way back to Subbstring, we are much closer than we thought."

Yes! I think to myself, and now with Hax's help I'm a step closer to getting the pills and helping my grandma!

We pack away my tent and get ready to get back to Subbstring. Grandma's already gone a day without her pills, I do hope she's ok, she has got to be right?

"Get on then Rocco," Hax says, tilting his head towards the wagon as he attaches Tori to it.

I place my foot onto a small step and jump in. The wagon is filled with a thin layer of snow, but that's ok, I guess. It's just a bit of frozen water.

I sit at the front as Hax jumps in, causing the wagon to shake a little.

"Go Tori!" he says and the cow starts trotting along through the white glazed woods, "Anyway, Rocco, what's the plan on how to get your Grandma's pills?"

Uh, I guess I never really had thought about what we were going to do.

"Well first we need to get my sledge back," I say, but I know how vague it is, it could have fallen off the gritting lorry anywhere between Subbstring and... wherever I was when I met Basset and Warwick.

"Well where is it?" Hax asks.

"I... I don't really know. But I'm sure we'll be able to..."

Hax raises his head high like a meerkat on look out. Had he heard something weird?

"Hax?"

"SSHHH!" he stares into the woods.

Tori stops and looks about, a worried look on her face. I lean towards her and start to stroke her back.

"It's ok," I whisper not knowing what was going on but acting calm.

Hax turns his head slowly to a bush.

"Hax?"

He panics and starts yelling.

"Tori go, TORI GO!"

The poor cow lashes out and starts running in circles! I panic too of course, what if the guy from the pub has been following us!

"NO TORI STRAIGHT!" Hax hollers.

"MOOOO!" The cow rears up onto her two back feet, sending me flying off the back of the waggon.

"AGH!" I scream as I land on my back in the cold snow.

"ROCCO!" Hax yells looking around and noticing my absence.

Tori spins around and I have to crawl out the way quickly before the hooves or wheels flatten me.

"WOAH!" I jump back, wandering what started all the commotion.

"MOO!" Tori jumps up again, flicking more snow onto me.

"Hey!" I get up and wipe the snow off me, "What was that.."

Before I can finish the wagon spins around and a piece of wood whacks me round the ribs.

"OUCH!" I groan, my feet flipping over my head and crashing to the ground, landing right next to a small grass snake.

Tori freezes and I hear Hax whisper;

"Rocco, don't move!"

I slowly get up.

"Hax, It's just a grass snake," I pick the little thing up and it curls its tail around my pinky finger, "It's tiny."

I show it to him with a slight smile.

"AGH! GET IT AWAY!"

"MOOO!"

The reaction takes me by surprise but it's a little bit funny.

"Hax," I say, putting the grass snake back onto the snow, "are you afraid of snakes?"

He gets up and brushes the snow off his jacket.

"No," He says with a cough, "No, Haha, Tori is."

I look at Tori and the little cow rolls her eyes. A giggle slips out before I can stop it and Hax flushes red.

But it's only then when I look around and notice, because of all that commotion there are pieces of wood everywhere, cracks in trees and skid marks in the mud and snow.

"Umm... Hax," I say anxiously, "I think the waggon is broken."

He looks around at all the wood chips on the floor.

"At least the main part is still standing."

There is a sudden crash noise and I take a deep intake of breath.

"Or maybe not."

Hax stands there awkwardly in the remains of the wagon that just completely snapped and fell in.

12

"What do we do now?" I ask, "That was our only transport!"

Hax sighs loudly.

"It's too far to walk, and I know Tori can't take both of our weight."

We look around for a bit, but I know it's hopeless, who else would be out here in the middle of the woods during a snow day!

"We could always fix it," I say, hanging on to the last hope we have of making it back home.

"I guess it's worth a shot," Hax replies, "We'll have to go find a lot of wood though."

"Well, you go that way, I'll go this way, get as much wood as we can carry," I smile and Hax does to.

"Good plan."

I walk into the woods, it is weird seeing everything like this, completely covered in milky white powder. I look about, there isn't much usable wood here, what was I thinking? We can't rebuild that wagon, it was old enough already.

I sit down against a tree and look at all the pearly snow drop flowers, sprouting out of the snowy ground. If we do get back to Subbstring, I am going to need my sledge. Where could it be though? I try to remember as much as I can about the morning I was being chased by Mrs Turnip. Mrs Turnip! That's it, if anyone has my sledge, that is where it will be.

I get up and begin walking back to the wagon when I hear something, it sounds like a voice. I kind of recognise it, a squeaky, high pitched voice.

"Kid, kid, where are you?!"

"You know he won't come when your calling him 'kid' and not his name."

"Oh yeah, right. What was his name again?"

"It was Rocco, you pea-brained idiot!"

"Oh yeah, right! ROCCO, ROCCO!"

I spin around, it's Basset and Warwick! They found us! They can help us get back!

I sprint through the bushes and trees until I get to a large blackberry bush. I peer through it and can see two rather differently shaped figures.

"Ugh, Basset I'm cold," one squeaked.

"Oh, stop complaining Warwick! You're wearing a scarf and bobble hat! Rocco is out there alone!"

I can't help myself.

"WARWICK, BASSET!" I yell, bursting through the bushes, sending the snow that had settled on top falling to the ground.

They both jump and turn to face me, Bassets jaw dropped.

"Rocco!" He says with a gasp, "We found you!"

I hug them both as they try to ask me questions.

"Ok, ok," I say, cutting them off, "long story short me and my friend Hax need help getting back to Subbstring as soon as possible."

There is a pause as the two of them exchange a look and a sigh.

"Ok," says Basset, "We'll help you, but only because it's cold out here and we were worried about you!"

I sprint back through the woods, Basset and Warwick at my side trying to keep up.

"Can we slow down a bit," Warwick puffs, "You're going too fast."

I let out a small laugh as he grabs the side of his stomach and gallops like an injured pony.

We burst through the leaves to find Tori slowly plodding around the ruins of the wagon.

"Tori!" I say, running up to her and giving her a stroke, "Is Hax back yet?"

"MOOO!"

"Ah, Ok," I lean in and whisper to Basset, "this is Hax's cow."

I can tell that he's confused, but I try to ignore it.

"Rocco!"

Hax comes bursting through some bushes.

"Hax!"

"I couldn't find any loose pieces of wood that weren't attached to a tree," he says sadly.

"Don't worry," I reply, nodding at Warwick and Basset, "These are my friends, they said they could give us a lift!"

Hax lets out a long sigh of relief.

"Thank you so much."

13

I sit in the middle seat of Basset and Warwick's gritting lorry as we all drive back to Subbstring. I'm so glad they gave us a lift, I was beginning to think we would be stuck there for ever!

"Just take one more left and you'll be entering Subbstring," Hax instructs from the back, there weren't enough seats for him and he balanced out the weight being at the back.

Hax taps me on the shoulder.

"So," he says in a whisper, "Where do you think your sledge would be?"

"I think Mrs Turnip has it," I reply quietly.

Hax's eyes widen and he exchanges a worried look with Tori.

"Is something wrong?"

"No," Hax replies, almost trying to cover something up, "it's just... Mrs Turnip isn't... the nicest person ever. She is always threatening to sue my DIY Shop just because she can't reach the top shelf!"

I smile.

"Subbstring!" squeaks Warwick as we pass under a wooden gate.

I turn back to stare out of the windscreen! Yes! We made it!

"Where abouts do you want us to stop?" Basset asks, pulling up near my Grandma's house.

"NOT THERE!" I quickly shout, "sorry, if my Grandma sees me, she won't let me get her pills, and we really need to get them!"

Basset doesn't say anything, he just drives a little further and stops us off near Hax's DIY Shop.

"Is here good?" he asks, opening the one door with his hand, the other with his foot as he stretches across me and Warwick.

I don't hesitate, I just jump out the door, eager to get those pills! My feet sink in the snow, it is even thicker over here!

"Good luck Rocco!" Warwick squeaks as Basset gets Hax and Tori out of the back.

The three of them walk over to me, their boots also sinking in the high snow.

"Rocco," says Basset, tapping me on the shoulder.

I spin around and he hands me a small piece of paper. My face turns from happy to confused in an instant. He smiles.

"It's my phone number," he says, "in case you need help."

Basset jumps back into the lorry and drives off.

"Good luck kid!"

I stand next to Hax and Tori, staring at the almost deserted Subbstring, it looks different like this, all layered with pearly white snow.

"C'mon," Hax says, beginning to walk down the road, "I have a plan!"

We stumble through the streets before arriving at Mrs Turnips house.

"MOOO!"

"Shhhhh Tori!" I say, covering her snout with my hand, "Let's go around the back."

I look at Hax and he follows swiftly.

The three of us quickly run behind the house, as quietly as we could but no matter what the snow still crunched beneath us. I lean against the wall and can see the area of ruined ground where my sledge had flattened it yesterday.

"Is she in?" Hax asks me as he too leans against the wall.

A take a step out and scour all the windows. Wow, she must have like five floors and lots of windows! There is a window open on the second floor, but I can't see her through it. Not on the third, fourth. Aha! That's when I see an elderly woman slowly hobble past a fifth-floor window.

"Yeah she is!" I say running back to Hax and Tori.

"What's the plan then," Hax whispers, "How do we get in?"

I look back up at the open window on the second floor.

"Ok," I say, "so Hax, if you boost me on your shoulders, I think I can just reach the window up there."

Hax looks up at the window.

"Yeah but what about Mrs Turnip?" Hax whispers, "She's bound to notice you!"

Agh, I didn't think of that!

"If only there was someone who could distract her!"

Hax exchanges a look with Tori and she slowly trots towards me. My jaw drops, how is a cow going to distract someone?

"How?" I ask, completely confused.

Hax smiles.

"You'll see."

Tori gallops over to Mrs Turnip's front door and kicks it with her hoof.

"COMING!" I hear Mrs Turnip yell in her so obviously fake nice voice.

I can't help but peer over the edge of the house just to see what Tori will do!

Mrs Turnip opens the door to see the cow standing there.

"Ummm... can I help you?"

Tori looks over and gives me a wink. And that's when she begins. The black and white patched cow jumps up onto her back legs and starts... Irish tap dancing?

I silently laugh, this is the funniest thing ever! A cow, standing on her back legs, her front legs on her hips, doing a little tango. I can't see Mrs Turnip, but I can imagine the confused expression.

Tori suddenly jumps up and bashes her hooves together, apparently this is called a Treble Jig!

Hax grabs my shoulder.

"C'mon!" He says.

We turn away from Tori and hurry under the window.

"Ok," I say, "how are we going to do this?"

"Ummm," he looks up at the window, then back down at me, "I'll crouch down."

He bends over and I jump onto his back, then crawl up onto his shoulders.

"Ok," He grunts, slowly standing up.

"Woah!"

I try to stay balanced, who knew it would be this hard!

"Now just grab the windowsill!" Hax says, slightly tipping to the side.

"Ok…"

I take a deep breath, I can do this. I reach my arms up and grip the edge of the windowsill. Ok, I've got it, now I just need to… I slowly pull myself towards the top and, I'm up!

I sit in the windowsill. I actually did it!

"I'm up!" I shout down to Hax.

"Great!" He yells back, "Now go get your sledge!"

I hop off the window and into the house. What on earth, this woman is crazy! The carpet is bright pink, her couch is white and the walls are a pastel magenta. It's like an atomic bomb of pink has just gone off in here. How weird is it that her attitude is so grumpy and inhumane but then her house is so perky and bright.

I run through the cream coloured door and into a kind of balcony like area with stairs going up and down. I decide to go up, if she was to hide my sledge, it would be in the attic.

The stairs are carpeted and remind me of the colour of a wild pig, now I see the resemblance! Anyway, I dash up a few stairs when I see a small window. I peak through and see that Tori is still doing a little jig, her arms and udders flailing around. But Mrs Turnip looks like she's about to give up! I need to hurry.

There is one more flight of stares and I've made it to the attic. I burst through the door and am completely shocked; It's a mess! How can the rest of her house be so tidy and perfect, then up here have everything from a walking stick collection and a half eaten pizza on the floor. But my eyes are suddenly drawn to the bright red sledge on the top of a completely over flowing cupboard! Yes, it *is* here!

I slowly make my way towards it, trying not to make a noise that Mrs Turnip will hear. I push through a pile of socks and just manage to get to the cupboard. Right, how do I do this, I think. I need to try to… just… grab it! I jump for it, but miss, landing on the side of my foot, making me fall over, my hand smacking onto an old stereo.

"Near, far, where ever you are. I believe that..."

I quickly try to grab the stereo and muffle the sound. Where's the off button!

"My heart will go onnnnnn..."

It won't stop playing Titanic! Mrs Turnip is bound to hear it.

"SHUT UP!" I yell at it, trying to find an off switch.

"Once more, you open the door..."

Agh! I try pressing every button, panicking completely. It has to be one of these. Finally, I find the off button and the music slowly stops. Phew, that was close!

I try again, one... two... three... and jump! My fingers slightly scrape the sledge, but not enough to knock it down. That's when an idea hits me. The walking stick collection! I grab one of the walking sticks and reach up to the top of the cupboard, my tiptoes giving me a slight boost. I get the walking stick behind it and fling the sledge to the floor.

It crashes loudly and I gasp! Did Mrs Turnip notice? I pick up the sledge beneath my arm and run down the stairs to a small window. No, Mrs Turnip is still watching as Tori starts doing the YMCA. Ok, I just need to get back to Hax.

In a hurry, I run down the stairs, trying not to be to loud at the same time. But then, disaster strikes, I trip over my feet half way down the stairs, and tumble the rest of the way down.

"AGH!" I groan.

I hit the floor and come to a stop, I feel dizzy and am starting to see stars. My head aches and I really hope Mrs Turnip didn't hear my quick shriek.

That's when I notice the photo frame I had knocked off on the way down. Uh oh, I hope it's not smashed! I run over to it and pick it up. I can't believe it, my whole body goes cold, in this photo, with the words;

Me and my grandson engraved onto it.

The photo shows Mrs Turnip, with her arms rapped around the guy from the pub! The one who first noticed me! The one who Hax believed planned my parent's death! Mrs Turnip is his Grandmother!

I put the painting down, drenched in shock. This whole time! And just as I think things can't get worse, I hear Mrs Turnip walk through the door, yelling at Tori to go away.

I panic and run through a door, into the same room with the open window.

"Is someone there?" Mrs Turnip's fowl voice comes from the other room.

I run to the window, my heart racing quicker than ever.

"HAX!" I whisper while trying not to yell.

He isn't there! Where is he!

"YOU!"

I spin around to see Mrs Turnip standing in the doorway.

"HOW DARE YOU BREAK INTO MY HOUSE!"

I have no choice, as Mrs Turnip runs at me, I chuck the sledge out the window and jump right out after it!

"AAGH!" I scream as I fall through the air.

I have to try to aim to land in that thick pile of snow. I close my eyes, too scared of the ground and…

"UGH!"

I land on my front in the freezing snow, but on the bright side, I'm not dead! I get up, look up at the window and see Mrs Turnip glaring at me.

"I'M GONNA GET YOU THIS TIME KID!"

She runs off, I know she'll be outside in a second, so I grab my sledge, place it the right way up, and jump on it, sliding down to the street.

My heart is racing, that was close, but it's not over yet. I slide down the bank, speeding up towards the road.

"ROCCO!"

I shoot past Hax, he must have gone to check on Tori just as I needed him! There's a loud slam noise from behind me and I know Mrs Turnip has just got out her house.

"YOU!" Her voice hollers from behind me, she must have noticed Hax.

I reach the road. It's best not to look back, I know I should probably wait for Hax, but I need to get to the pharmacy as quick as I can, he'll understand.

<u>14</u>

The snow lashes at my face as I continue to ride down the road. It's snowing hard now, first I wanted snow, but now it just gets in the way. The houses and shops are a blur due to the amount of snow falling and the speed I'm going. That's when I notice, how quick am I going? I can barely see through the snow, and it feels like I'm going too fast, can this plastic sledge hold out? I laugh, I'm being stupid, it's what sledges are made for! Anyway, where abouts is the pharmacy again? Oh right, just down the…

"WATCH OUT!"

A girl jumps out the way and I smash through a glass window, jumping off my sledge as I fall onto a tiled floor of one of the isles in the supermarket.

I lie there, completely aching. What just happened? I wasn't paying attention; I must have run right into our local food store! I can feel a small cut on my right cheek where some of the glass scratched me, and my leg is killing me.

"Oh my word, are you ok?!"

The same voice who yelled watch out ran next to me and grabbed my arm.

"Ok," she says, "Oh god, you're bleeding, don't worry."

She helps me up and we come face to face. I know her! She goes to my school. She's about my height, maybe a bit taller, my age as well. She's slightly Asian looking, with amber to gold ombre hair that goes down to her knees.

"Rocco?" she says, recognising me, "what were you doing?"

"No time to explain," I say, taking a step forward.

My knee buckles under the pressure when I'm off her grip and I fall to the floor.

"Oh my god, Rocco, you're hurt!" she says, kneeling down to help me up again.

"Really Fleur, I'm fine," I don't want to be rude, but a sore knee isn't going to stop me from getting the pills.

"You're obviously not fine," She says, putting a tissue to my bleeding cheek, "come back to mine, we'll get you a first aid kit."

I grab my sledge and Fleur helps me hobble out the shop and towards her house. At first, I just wanted to get to the pharmacy, but my mind has just drifted to my aching leg.

We arrive at her house, it's about the same size as my grandma's but isn't as overgrown with ivy. She takes me along the foot path and to the front door which she quickly knocks on.

"Thanks for this Fleur," I say, still focused on my leg.

"Don't worry," she says with a smile, "anyway, I kind of feel like it's my fault you went through the glass."

Her Mum open's the door, it's weird, she looks exactly like Fleur but just taller.

"Hi honey," her mum says, only noticing me afterwards, "Oh, who's this?"

"Mum, no time to explain, this is Rocco, and he's really hurt," Fleur replies quickly.

"Oh dear!"

I'm rushed inside and her mum lets me sit on a chair.

"What's wrong love?" she asks me.

I don't really know what to say.

"well, it's my leg," I reply, "it really hurts!"

"Let's have a quick looksie," her mum says with a smile, slowly rolling up my snowy trouser leg, "oooh."

I look down and it's slightly swollen, the colour however is black and about twenty shades of purple.

"Fleur, honey, would you go get some ice," Fleur runs out the room and her mum turns to me, "should I call your parents?"

Her words take me by shock.

"NO!" I reply quickly, "Sorry, she... she already knows."

I look over at Fleur standing in the doorway, she's staring at me and I know she knows I'm lying. Her mum looks at her and she walks over with the ice.

"Yeah," Fleur says, "we stopped off at the telephone box and told his Grandma what happened."

Phew. I want to thank her for not ratting me out, but not while her mum's here.

"Ah," her mum says, "I'm just going to get some tissues, you hold the ice to your leg."

Her mum slowly leaves the room and I take my chance on thanking Fleur.

"Thanks for not telling your mum that my Grandma doesn't know," I say.

"No problem," she replies, sitting on the table next to me.

"Quick question, what were you doing outside the store?"

"Oh," she smiles, "I was just getting some food for the evening."

I look confused as we both know it was closed.

"Fine," she says with a sigh, "so I may have been nicking a packet of crisps."

I laugh, you would think I'd be angry, but the truth is, I was planning to steal the pills if the pharmacy wasn't open. There is a slam of the door and her mum walks back in with some bandages and fastens the all ice pack to my leg. It relieves a lot of the pain.

"Thank you," I say.

She smiles

"No problem."

15

I spend about an hour at Fleur's house, my leg slowly feeling better, her mum reckoned I had sprained it, but I was just worried about getting to the pharmacy. I should really have waited for Hax, then we could have got the pills by now, and I wouldn't have sprained my leg while vandalising a shop at the same time. That reminds me, I should probably be getting back on track.

"Thank you for this," I say to Fleur and her mum, "But I should probably be getting back to my Grandma's house."

"Ok," her mum says with a warm smile, "you should come visit sometime."

I smile and get up slowly, my leg feeling much better. Fleur looks at me suspiciously, I wonder if she knows I'm not really going back to my Grandma's house.

"Thanks again," I say as I pick up my sledge and walk out the front door.

I'm about half way down the driveway, my sledge scraping along the snowy ground, when Fleur bursts through the front door. I spin around to see her standing there with a blue scarf on.

"Where are you really going Rocco," she says once the door is closed.

"What do you mean?" I reply, acting dumb.

"You can't hide it," she says, "I know you're not going back to your Grandma's."

I sigh.

"Fine," I think about telling her, after all she's done for me, it's the least I can do, "I'm going to get my Grandma's pills from the pharmacy, she needs them to stay well, and she can't just go without them."

She stares at me, obviously thinking hard.

"I'll go with you," she declares, walking out of the doorway and coming towards me.

This makes me think, should I let her come, she would come in handy.

"Fine," I say, she smiles and joins my side, "Let's go!"

We walk out of her front gates and through the streets, they are completely deserted, the wind howling and snow swirling around them.

"Where abouts is the pharmacy?" Fleur asks, her hair catching every drop of snow.

We stop.

"I think it's just down the slope, next to where the Christmas Tree was," I reply, at least that was where I remember it being.

"Ok."

It started snowing harder again, a complete storm even. Rock hard snow chipping away at us as we tried to make our way down the street. The wind roars louder than an earth quake, tugging at every loose piece of clothing and hair we have. I look over at Fleur, I can tell she's struggling to fight against the sheer coldness of the weather.

"Maybe we should turn back?" she shouts, the wind taking her voice away.

I look down the road at the blurry village.

"We're closer to the pharmacy then we are to your house!" I reply.

She closes her eyes and nods. We continue to go against the strength of the wind, it's almost like someone was tying ropes around us and pulling us backwards, up into the snowy grey clouds.

There's a sudden loud crack sound and I look at Fleur, she looks back and we both stare up at the telephone poll.

"RUN!" I yell.

She screams and we sprint down the road, with the wind still against us, the telephone pole collapsing over us.

"AAAAGH!"

The huge wooden pole hits the ground just behind me, snapping and sending pieces of wood flying.

"GET DOWN!" Fleur shouts.

I turn around to see a piece of wood flying towards me, I jump out the way as quick as I can, landing face first into a pile of snow.

I sigh a sigh of relief and push myself up, out of the snow and brush the flakes off my coat.

"Are you Ok?" Fleur asks, walking over to me.

"Yeah," I reply.

16

We both turn around at the same time and stare at the completely splintered remains of the telephone pole in the snow.

"Woah," Fleur exclaims with a gasp, "that was close!"

"Yeah," I say, out of breath.

The storm is still raging around us. I can barely feel my ears and fingers through all the cold.

"We should get going," I say, pointing towards the snow coloured building with a green cross on the front, "It'll be safer in there."

"Ok," she replies and we continue to make our way towards it.

We make it to the pharmacy, wind striking us as we go. I run up to the door and try to open it. My hands shake the doorknob for a few seconds before I give up.

"It's locked," I shout over the wind.

Fleur looks up and down at the door and the rectangular shaped windows next to it.

"Stand back," she says, running off into the deserted car park.

I do what she says and get out of the way, confused. What is she doing? Is she just leaving?

"HEADS!" she yells, I duck out the way and she comes running at full speed towards the door, then chucks a rock at the window.

There's a loud crack sound as the rock smashes through the glass, completely breaking the window. I look at her in disbelief, in school she was known as the goody-goody.

"C'mon then," she says as if it was nothing, slowly stepping through the broken window.

I hesitate, then follow her, carefully stepping over the jagged glass. As soon as I'm inside the warmth heats up my entire body, comforting and healing my frost-bite-feeling. I decide to drop my sledge next to a plant pot.

"Ok," I say, looking around, "We need to try to find my Grandma's pills."

"Well, what are they?" Fleur asks, going behind the front counter and opening drawers.

"I'll recognise them once I see them."

I look around the reception for a bit, but then decide to try a different room.

"C'mon," I say to Fleur, pushing open a door into a room with a bunch of chairs in rows.

"This must be the waiting room," she says, stepping in and looking around.

It's completely dark, you can only make out a few objects.

"Are there any lights?" I ask, tripping over a chair leg.

"No," Fleur replies, "It'll just show that we're in here."

I nod, she is right, we are not meant to be here. There is a rustle sound and my eyes are drawn to the darkest corner of the room.

"Did you hear that?" I whisper, fixed on the dark corner.

"Hear what?"

I step a bit closer.

"Is someone there?" I call, my voice echoing in the obviously empty room.

"Rocco," Fleur says, standing next to me, "there's no one there."

I look at her. I guess it was just a random noise from the loud storm outside. But it sounded like someone quickly dashing out of the way, no, it can't be, I'm being silly.

"Ok," I say, turning back to Fleur slowly, "the pills aren't here, let's look in another room."

"Alright," she walks out, back into reception.

I don't follow her, I just stare at the dark corner. I have the weird feeling that I'm being watched, that a pair of eyes are following my every move.

"Coming?" she asks, opening the door again.

"Yeah," I say and I turn back around, walking out the door she is holding open.

We walk back into the reception and think for a bit.

"Where would they keep the pills?" I ask myself.

"Maybe here," I turn around to see Fleur standing next to two doors, "I mean, they are the only two other rooms."

I walk towards her, it's hard to see anything in the darkness of the pharmacy. I think about the lights again, but then come to the conclusion that the power is also out. The pills are behind one of these doors, I think, I push against one but it's like pushing against the wall itself.

"Locked," I say with a sigh.

"Well there has to be a key somewhere?" Fleur walks behind the front desk, "maybe in these drawers."

She goes through them again, I join her. The drawers are old and they make a screech sound as we open them. I slowly open one and there is a packet of gum and a torch. Maybe this could come in handy.

"I found this," I say, turning on the torch and shining it at the doors.

It reveals two signs;

DOCTOR'S ROOM

MEDICINE STORAGE

"Well that's got to be where they are kept," I say, shaking the torch light around the sign.

"Yeah," Fleur says, looking at the sign with concentration.

I try another drawer and there's a polaroid picture of two children laughing. Not like that would help us. I sigh and open the last one, my hopes fading.

My face lights up! Sitting in the bottom of the wooden drawer is a small key labelled; MEDICINE STORAGE ROOM.

"I've got it!" I say, holding it up in excitement.

"Yes!" Fleur jumps happily, "chuck me the torch!"

I throw the torch and she catches it, then I run to the Storage door, heart pounding with glee. Fleur shines the light on the keyhole so I can see as I insert the key and slowly twist it. I wait for a few long dead seconds, then hear two clicks and the door swings open.

"YES!" I yell and give her hi-five.

<u>17</u>

We both walk in, Fleur hands me the torch and I shine it around. The room is filled with shelves, shelves so high that they nearly touch the roof.

"Woah," I gasp, "this place is huge!"

Fleur looks at me, worried.

"Rocco, how on earth are we meant to find a certain packet of pills in all this!"

Ah, she's right, there must be close to fifty shelves in here!

"Well," I say, "the pills are yellow, and they have a yellow and white carboard box," I say, trying to remember the image of the pills in Grandma's cupboard.

"Ok," she says, "We'll split up."

"But we only have one torch?" I say.

"We'll manage."

She runs down a different aisle. It is lighter in this room than the others. I slowly walk down the aisle, looking at all the different medicines and pills. I can't believe this journey is coming to an end, I mean I'm so glad I can finally give my Grandma the pills, but it's been an adventure I'll never forget.

I stumble along, shining my torch up and down, looking at every small rectangular shaped box. What if they don't even have the pills? What if after all this, they are not even in stock! I'm panicking, I tell myself, I just need to calm down, of course they'll be here.

"ROCCO?!"

I spin around to the sound of Fleur's voice.

"I THINK I FOUND THEM!"

I run down the aisles, so excited. My feet pounding on the floor, my heart racing. She's not in this aisle, or this one. I stop and see her staring at the lowest shelf.

"FLEUR!" I yell, running towards her and sliding to a stop.

I look at the pills, breathing heavily. They look right, I read the label;

MEN'S HAIR GROWTH TABLETS

"Agh," Fleur says with a sigh, "sorry, I couldn't read the label in the dark."

"It's ok," I say, my heart sinking into my shoes, "Let's just keep looking."

We can't give up, not now. I've come too far for there to be nothing here. I walk on into a different aisle, disappointed but still persevering as I try to find the pills.

What if there was only one packet left and they were sold before the snow day, I should have bought some pills rather than my sledge on the way back from school. But I guess the rat would just have eaten those ones anyway.

Not expecting to find anything, I shine my torch onto the top row of boxes.

"Wart remover, no. Eyes drops, no." I read them out as I go along, making sure I don't miss it, "Calpol, no. Lung pills for senior citizens, no, wait? YES!"

I shine my torch on the yellow and white packets, almost jumping for joy!

"FLEUR! I'VE GOT THEM! FLEUR, FLEUR!"

I hear her pounding footsteps as she dashes towards me.

"You do?!" She says in shock, standing next to me.

"Up there!" I say, pointing to the container.

"How do we get up there though," she asks.

I didn't think of that.

"There has to be a ladder somewhere," I say, "How would the employees get to it?"

We look about for a second but it doesn't take long until we come across a huge metal ladder on small wheels.

"Ok," Fleur says, "You take that side, I'll take this side."

I walk to the side she's pointing at and we start pushing it down the aisles. It's quite heavy, I'm sure we'll get there in the end, but it makes an ear-splitting screech as we move it.

"Just one more push," I say as we shove it in line with the pills.

"Ok," she says, "You climb up and grab the pills."

I don't need telling twice, I quickly climb up the ladder, thinking about my Grandma and the joyful look on her face when I hand her the pills.

I get to the top and suddenly hear the sound of a door slamming shut. I instantly look down at Fleur, worried.

"What was that?" I shout down.

"No idea," she replies, "I'll go check it out!"

She runs towards the now open door and I get back on track. I can see the pills just a block away from me. Just a short reach away. I stretch out my arm and my fingers just slightly touch the box. My toes are the only thing stabilising me as I spread my entire body out, trying to reach.

"AGH!" I scream and it echoes through the room as I lose my balance and start to fall, luckily, I catch the metal shelf below with my gripping fingers.

I'm breathing heavily, petrified of the fall beneath my dangling feet. Just one push! I use my energy to swing my hand around and knock the pills over, sending them crashing to the ground.

That's fine I think, I can just get them when I get back down, it's how I get down I'm focusing on right now. I try swinging my legs to the ladder, but that doesn't work. Ok, maybe I can just... I shimmy my hands along trying to get to the ladder, my hands sweating and aching.

I'm much closer now, just one more...

My feet hit the ladder and I can finally breathe out. Phew, that was close. I climb down the ladder quickly and pick up the pills, just the feel of them in my hands makes me happy. I've done it!

There is another door slam noise and I hear Fleur scream. I jump around, I had forgotten about Fleur!

"FLEUR!" I yell.

"ROCC..."

I run down the aisles, trying to find her, but she's no where to be seen!

"FLEUR!" I yell again, this time there is no response.

I spin around after hearing the sound of footsteps, I'm not the only one here.

"Rocco..." It's not Fleur's voice, it's a man's.

I turn around, staring down one of the aisles to see a dark figure walking towards me. I shine my torch on it and gasp. Standing there, face illuminated by the light, is the same man who noticed me in the pub, Mrs Turnip's grandson. And he's got one bulky arm wrapped around Fleur.

"WHERE IS HE!" the man yelled.

"Where's who?" I say.

"YOU KNOW," the man hollers. "THE ONE WHO KILLED YOU PARENTS!"

"THAT WAS YOU!" I shout back, suddenly filled with anger.

He shakes his head.

"No, my boy, I'm Clinton, one of your Dad's best friends."

One of my Dad's best friends?

"WHAT RUBBISH!" I yell at him, "JUST LET GO OF FLEUR AND RUN OFF!"

"NOT TILL YOU GIVE ME HIM!"

"WHO!"

"THE ONE WHO CAUSED THE CAR CRASH YOUR PARENTS WERE IN, THE PERSON WHO MURDERED CAIN AND SASHA!"

"THAT WAS YOU," I scream, "DON'T LIE!"

"No Rocco, the person who killed your parents… was Hax."

18

These words take me back. Hax, the one who caused my parents death? Who murdered them when I was two? Surely not, I think.

"We were best friends, me, your parents and Hax. But Hax loved Sasha, and Sasha chose Cain over him. So, one night, when they were driving home Hax through a piece of wood he had got from a tree that day into the road, it hit Cain's tyres and the car flipped over. Hax only meant to injure them, he never told any one it was him, but I always knew, that he was the one who caused the car crash and Cain and Sasha's death," says Clinton.

I collapse into tears. I trusted Hax, and he lied to me. Was he just helping me out through guilt, or was he helping me just to cover up his deeds? Hax told me that Clinton caused the car crash to cover it up, so was this whole thing just a cover up.

Clinton lets go of Fleur and she runs over to give me a hug.

"I'm so sorry Rocco," she says.

"Yeah," Clinton walks towards us, "you shouldn't have had to find out this way."

I'm breathing heavily, completely taken back by the news. There is a long silence as Fleur pats me on the back and Clinton stares at me in awe.

"CLINTON!"

I get up and the three of us spin around to see Hax standing in the door way.

"Hax?" I say, full of anger now, "HAX IS THIS TRUE!"

Hax looks at the floor.

"Yes."

I'm breathing heavily, feeling like a bull ready to go on a rampage.

"AAAGHHHH!" I run towards Hax and he grabs my arm and holds it against my back.

"No one is going to find out," Hax growls evilly, "I can't let you go back to your Grandma and tell her what happened."

A bucket of fear is thrown on me, completely drenching me in anxiety.

"Hax, please?" I whimper.

"ROCCO!" Fleur cries as Hax pushes me to the ground.

"You to *girl*," Hax sneers, running over to her.

How could this be happening!

"Don't touch her!" Clinton shouts, stepping in front of Fleur.

I'm worried for Clinton, Hax is no longer a happy cuddly bear, he's a vicious tiger, with no good intention.

"You know what," Hax says, slowly turn away from Clinton to face me, "I won't hurt her. She isn't the one who told Rocco my secret. YOU ARE!"

Hax spins around and punches Clinton in the chest, sending him flying to the shelf, completely knocking it over. Medicines spilling everywhere and pills rolling across the floor.

I gasp, Clinton is obviously out cold and he was the only one strong enough against Hax. The sound of my gasp makes Hax slowly turn back to me.

"Hax?" I ask, "are you really doing this?"

There is no answer, but I know the answer; the look in his eyes have changed. He struts towards me, filled with anger and pushes me to the ground.

I slide a bit, making the floor screech. Then there is a clunk sound and me and Hax both look at the packet of pills that fell out my pockets.

"NO!" I yell as Hax picks them up and slips them in his jacket pocket.

I get up and run towards Hax as he strides towards the door.

"GIVE THEM BACK!" I yell, gripping onto his arm.

He shakes me off and Fleur runs towards him.

"THEY ARE NOT YOURS!" she shouts, slapping him around his large stomach.

Hax grunts and bends down, grabbing Fleur's ankle, then stands up again, holding her upside down.

"LET GO OF ME!" she screams, trying to punch him with her flailing arms, "ROCCO!"

I'm completely frozen in fear as Hax runs out the room.

Completely filled with shock, I chase after him, bursting through the door, into the reception. It's deserted, not a sign of Hax or Fleur. This is not happening, Hax has taken the pills and Fleur!

"FLEUR!" I shout, running into the waiting room.

They're not in here either. It's just an empty room with chairs and magazines. I storm out, back into the reception. I stare at the broken window I came through and run back out, into the snowy village.

The snow swirls around me. Hax is gone with the pills and he has kidnapped Fleur! What am I going to do!

19

C'mon Rocco think! Think! If I were Hax, where would I go. Then it hits me, I have a plan. I run back inside, get my sledge and place it on the snow outside. I take a deep breath and jump on. It's the third time I've used this sledge, let's hope the saying third time lucky is actually true.

As I glide down the snowy streets I know exactly where to go, if this plan is going to work, I'm going to need to take a short cut, and that's through the woods I was told never to go in.

I slide towards the main road, but turn off into the winter woods. I have to be careful not to slide into the white glazed trees. The sledge takes me into the path of some cream coloured rabbits that scatter as I swish past.

I'm ready now, ready to get those pills, ready to reveal the truth about my parents, and ready to save Fleur from Hax.

I lean out of the way of a tree and then go flying over a small ditch that used to be a river. I can hear the birds screaming as they fly out of the trees when I zoom past. I think I've got the hang of sledging now, and I'm getting used to the cold of the snow.

I come out of the trees and I'm back in another part of the village, it was a good short cut, otherwise I would have still been near the telephone pole.

The buildings are coated in snow so it's hard to see the one I need. I come to a stop at the pavement, get off my sledge and look at the different shops.

I'm pretty sure that's the bakery, and I definitely don't think a loaf of bread will help me. I walk for a bit, then find a small shop with the picture of a dog on the window. Perfect! It's the pet store. Now it's just how to get in. Is it worth trying the door?

I slowly reach out and twist the doorknob, there is a click sound and it opens. Yes! Some employee must have forgotten to lock it. I walk in, cold and covered in snowflakes. Now what I need to get from here will help me a lot. I walk along the aisles till I find it, its red, black and yellow stripes make it so easy to spot.

I take a dog bone from a different aisle and use it to smash the glass, then slowly take out the animal.

"Ok," I say to it, "Let's just put you right in here."

I put it in a small plastic bag I found near the tills. I smile, it's all working to plan, I'll have my Grandma's pills back in no time!

I walk back outside, into the cold winter air. I look around at the shops, mist coming out my mouth when I breath, then slowly disappearing into the bleak air.

First, I put the plastic bag on the sledge, then I sit down and rap my legs around it so it doesn't come flying off. Sitting on the sledge, I reach out for the side of the pavement, then push myself off, head down the road and to the DIY shop, if Hax is anywhere, it would be there.

I glide down the street I walked along the day before the snow came, it all looks so different now. My legs grip tight around the bag, I can't let this fall off.

My sledge scrapes across the snow as I start to see the corner of the DIY shop between two buildings. I slip through and come to a stop just outside the rickety old building with the DIY sign about to fall off.

I get up, grab the plastic bag and leave my sledge there as I storm through the door.

"HAX!" I shout as the small bell chimes.

There is a long pause, the shop seems to be deserted, but the lights are on so I know it can't be.

"Rocco?"

Hax's voice comes from another room. I get ready, clutching the bag in my hands.

"Rocco is that you?" Hax comes through the door, carrying some boxes.

I don't hesitate, I take the small corn-snake out the bag and chuck it at him. He's afraid of snakes isn't he!

The black, red and yellow snake flings through the air and smacks around Hax's face.

"SNAKE!" Hax yells, chucking the boxes, sending nails and bolts flying everywhere.

I duck out the way and two nails stick into the wall behind me.

"ROCCO HELP!" Hax hollers, the snake crawling over him, covering his eyes as he runs around the shop aimlessly.

My plan is actually working.

"Not till you give me the pills, and let Fleur go!" I say in pride.

"WHO'S FLEUR?!" Hax replies, stumbling backwards and falling over the counter.

"Don't act dumb!" I shout, "The girl you kidnapped at the pharmacy!"

Hax runs from the counter, his arms flailing about. The snake hisses as it raps around his forehead and upper torso.

"When did I kidnap someone?!" Hax stumbles about, falling into a shelf and completely knocking it over.

It's like dominoes, each shelf falling over and knocking into the other. Paint, brooms, pots and pans all smash onto the floor, completely trashing the place.

I look back in shock. It's a mess! Well that's what he gets for lying!

"Just tell me where the pills and Fleur are!" I say, getting impatient.

Hax stands up and the snake falls to the ground, slithering under the mess of the shelves. He faces me, breathing heavily.

"Rocco, I don't know anyone called Fleur, why would I take your grandma's pills, and why on earth did you throw that snake at me when you know I hate them?" he asks

I pause and loosen up. What? But I know Hax was there!

"Hax, I was in the pharmacy getting the pills with my friend. We met the man from the pub there, apparently his name was Clinton. He told me that you were the one who killed my parents, then you appeared, knocked out Clinton, took the pills, and kidnapped Fleur," it all slides out of me so quickly, I'm just confused.

Hax stares at me, he looks just as confused as I am.

"Rocco, I wasn't there, I was here the whole-time putting Tori into the stables out back," Hax's words confuse me more.

"Then who was it?" I ask, it doesn't add up!

"Hang on," Hax says, "did you say Clinton from the pub was there?"

"Yeah..."

Hax gasps and runs to the counter and opens a drawer. He takes out a small picture and shows it to me. The picture shows a man and a woman, Hax and Clinton, all wearing their graduation gowns. I know instantly who the man and woman are, it's my parents.

"Hax..." I say, "you were also friends with Clinton?"

"Yeah," Hax replies, holding his head low, "Everyone called him Clint, he was one of our friends in secondary and university. But he would always get angry and overly jealous, he had a terrible lack of work ethic, the only thing he was really good at was drama. Clint was also clever though, he became an accountant with your dad, but then your dad was forced to fire him. Your dad didn't want to fire Clint, but he had to, as he kept slacking off. That must've enlightened Clint's anger to cause the car cash, and then come back for you!"

I step back, this all so much to take in, first it was Clint, then it was Hax, now it's Clint again!

"How can I believe you?!" I ask, "Clint told me it was you, then you showed up! I saw you there!"

"Rocco! It wasn't me!"

I sigh, I believe him, he's never given me a reason not to.

"But then who was it who took the pills," I say, "I was convinced it was you!"

Hax stops still, drops the picture and stares out the window.

"He escaped?"

What?! What is Hax talking about? I watch him, confused and completely lost.

"Rocco," Hax turns to me, "my parents always told me that I had an almost identical cousin called Zammer! Zammer was a builder before he got into a gang fight and got sent to prison, he must've escaped with during all the commotion about the snow!"

I think for a bit, it all makes sense now! The only thing is, Hax the lumberjack, Zammer the builder, that family was great at naming. I laugh to myself and then get back on track with the adventure.

"Where would we find Zammer and Clint then?" I ask

Hax thinks for a bit, then looks at me.

"The house in the woods!"

20

I look at Hax, confused again.

"What house in the woods?" I ask.

Hax opens the back door and whistles loudly before turning back to me.

"Remember your Grandma told you never to go into the forest," I nod and he continues telling the story, "Well, that's because there is a run-down house in there where Clint lived, if they would be anywhere, they would be there!"

My excitement rises higher than the roof! We are finally going to get the pills, and save Fleur! Tori comes running through the door Hax whistled out of, she jingles her bell as if saying that she is ready for an adventure!

"Ok," says Hax, "The quicker we get to the house, the safer your friend Fleur is, and the quicker we can get the pills for your Grandma!"

Tori moos in agreement and I smile. The three of us get ready and walk outside, but before we do, I have an idea.

"Hax, can I use your phone for a second?" I ask.

Hax spins around.

"Yeah sure," he says, "but why?"

Let's hope this works. I reach in my snowy pocket and take out a piece of paper. I dial the number, then put the phone to my ear. It buzzes for a bit, then a low, grumbly voice answers.

"Hi," I say into the phone, "Is this Basset?"

Hax smiles and begins to strap stuff around Tori.

"Oh, it's the run-down house in the woods," I say into the phone, "You can, perfect! See you guys there!"

I put the phone onto the wall, we have back up now, and the three of us walk outside, into the snowy outdoors. It's getting dark, Fleur's mum will be wondering where she is, and soon my Grandma would have been two days without pills!

"Let's go!" I say and we walk down the snowy street, ready to take on Clint and Zammer.

We stumble along for a while, the snow spiralling through the village. It's cold and the sun is setting slowly, causing the sky to turn a faint orange.

We stop at a small ally way and Hax nods towards it, indicating us to go in. I follow him and Tori. It's darker between the two buildings, gloomier too.

The three of us walk on a little bit till I can see light at the other end, we will be coming out onto the street again soon. I make it to the end of the ally and peer around.

"You see me here, in the middle of Subbstring, an English town that is seeing snow for the first time, and tons of it in deed!" a voice comes from a group of people, each holding a camera apart from one tall blonde man who seemed to be being filmed.

I turn to face Hax.

"It's Dr Flibbertigibbet from Newsround!" I say, "They're filming the intense snow!"

"And?" Hax says, confused.

"Maybe he could help!" I know it's a far stretch, more than that, but if someone has close contact with the police, they could just be useful.

"Rocco, I don't know about that..."

I turn back to Hax.

"It's worth a try!"

I slowly walk down the pavement towards them.

"CUT!" I hear Dr Flibbertigibbet yell, "It's just snow, there is NOTHING COOL ABOUT IT!"

The film crew react quickly, I guess it's not the first time Dr Flibbertigibbet has lost it.

"H...have some water... sir," one of the camera crew say, giving him a plastic water bottle.

Dr Flibbertigibbet takes the water bottle, squeezes it, then chucks it at the man holding a huge white umbrella like thing.

"DON'T TRY TO BUTTER UP TO ME! I'm trying to be mad ok!"

He rolls onto the snowy floor, sulking. I stare at him, he's different to what everyone sees on tv.

"Excuse me," I say slowly, "Dr Flibbertigibbet?"

He turns around and stares at me.

"Kid if you want an autograph, I really can't be bothered right now!"

"Actually," I say, "Would you be interested in a real news story."

He immediately lifts his head to face me.

"I'm listening."

I tell him about Fleur, Zammer and Clint and he watches my every word like a baby hearing a nursery rhyme.

"How amazing," He says standing up, "I mean amazingly awful... come on crew, we have a real story to document!"

I run back to Hax and Tori, smiling.

"They'll catch us up for back up," I say.

Hax smiles and pats me on the head.

"Well done Rocco, now let's go! We need to hurry!"

We run across the street and between another two buildings, the snow crunching beneath our boots and the wind whistling loudly. We run out of the two buildings and quickly dash towards the woods I sledged through moments ago. If only I had come across this 'run down house', then I wouldn't have thrown the snake at Hax and destroyed his shop.

The woods would usually be dark, but the snow brightens everything up a bit. As we walk along the woods seem to change from nice snowy beech trees, into tall dark oak trees, still snowy, but much more intimidating. I slow down, this place is unsettling and spooky. I can tell that Hax is beginning to get a bit agitated. Even the snow feels colder around here.

There is a sound of a twig snap and Tori jumps high into the air, mooing loudly. I grab her and begin to stroke her, trying to calm her down.

"Are you ok Tori?" Hax asks, it's the first time he's spoken since we entered the woods, I guess it's going to be weird seeing Clint again.

"Where to now Hax?" I ask, still stroking Tori's back.

Hax looks around, there's a small slope on our left and I'm pretty sure that's where we need to go.

"Over this slope," Hax says, I knew it!

The three of us slowly climb up the slope, trying not to make a noise, or slip over in the snow. Once we get to the top we lie down on our stomachs in the cold snow and peer over the top.

As the slope goes down on the other side there is a small, old building, it isn't really a house, it's more of a shack. It's covered in moss, mould and snow, the wood is dark brown and almost every plank is either snapped or cracked. It's a rough two stories, with no doors just holes in the walls.

I look at Hax.

"What do we do now?"

21

We stare at the shack for a bit, wondering what do. We don't even know if they are in there.

"Look!" says Hax, pointing to a small window where a man that looks just like him stumbled past.

"Is that Zammer?" I ask.

"Obviously!"

Not obviously, I think, they basically look exactly alike! We wait for an idea, but none come, come on Rocco, think! There's a rustle from a bush near the building. My head raises like a meerkat. I give Hax a nudge and point to the snow topped bush. We both stare at it till a recognisable character jumps out with his camera crew.

"It's Dr Flibbertigibbet!" I say, "He'll make a perfect distraction!"

"And follow me as we near the house of a … murderer!" He exclaims, walking towards the shack, his camera crew following like lemmings.

"OI! WHAT YA DOING HERE!" Clint comes running out through a hole in the wall, "ZAMMER! WE HAVE SOME GUESTS!"

Zammer comes striding after and they glare at Dr Flibbertigibbet. They say somethings that I can't quite make out, then Clint gives Dr Flibbertigibbet a shove.

"C'mon," I say, turning back to Hax and Tori, "now's our chance!"

I get up and Hax does too.

"You stay here Tori," he says, then he turns back to me and we hurry down the slope, trying not to make a loud noise in all the snow.

"C'mon," I whisper.

We rush down the hill, then run around the back of the shack. I can hear Zammer and Clint arguing with Dr Flibbertigibbet. There is a small hole in the wall that I duck under and run through, slowly followed by Hax.

The inside is nearly as run down as the outside, plants are growing through the floor boards and there is a small patch of snow where it has fell through a hole in the ceiling.

"I bet Fleur is up there," Hax says, pointing to some old rickety stairs.

I nod and we begin to walk up them. There's a loud crack sound and one of the stairs snap. I let out a small scream and Hax grabs me just before I can fall down.

"Thanks," I whisper.

We make it to the top and there in the corner, under one patch of sunlight, is Fleur. She has her hands tied behind her back and has a piece of tape around her mouth.

"Fleur!" I say and her eyes move to me.

I walk over to her and quickly rip the tape off her.

"Rocco!" she says with a sigh, "Thank you so much, these people are crazy!"

"I know!" I say with a laugh, "do you know where the pills are?"

"I think that Zammer guy has them," she says, followed by a scream, "Rocco watch out!"
She points to Hax and I instantly know what she's thinking.

"I'm Hax," he says, "not Zammer, Zammer's beard is shorter!"

Well that's good to know, I think. Hax helps Fleur untie her hands and we begin down the stairs when someone stops us.

"Not so fast," says a crooked voice.

I gasp as Mrs Turnip walks up the stairs towards us. I knew she was evil!

"ZAMMMER, CLINT!" she yells, "WE'VE GOT THEM!"

Me, Hax and Fleur back into the corner.

"What do we do?" Fleur asks.

My heart is beating as Zammer and Clint walk up the stairs and join Mrs Turnip.

"So great to see you again Rocco," Zammer sneers.

Uh oh! We're done for! I close my eyes tight as they walk towards us. That's when I hear it, a faint grumbling noise. I know exactly what it is. I give Fleur and Hax a light nudge.

"On the count of three, duck," I say, "One… two… THREE!"

I fall to the floor, so does Fleur and Hax, as a huge gritting lorry comes bursting through the wall, sending pieces of wood flying everywhere.

"WOOHOOO!" I hear Warwick shout.

The huge lorry rams into Mrs Turnip, Zammer and Clint, sending them flying into the wall.

"Oh, my word!" Fleur gasps as the lorry smashes through the other side of the wall, landing on it's back in the snow.

The hole of the top floor is completely destroyed, Clint is lying on the ground outside, Mrs Turnip is on the front of the gritting lorry, and Zammer is propped up against one of the only walls that is still in one piece. I get up, so does Fleur and Hax. I stare at the damaged gritting lorry.

Suddenly Mrs Turnip wakes up just as Basset and Warwick start to get out the lorry.

"How dare you!" Mrs Turnip growls at them.

She runs towards Warwick, swings him around, then chucks him to the snowy floor. I watch them in awe, they're having a full-on fight. Basset ducks as Mrs Turnip swings her walking stick at him.

"MOOOO!" Tori suddenly comes running down the hill at full speed.

Mrs Turnip's scream fills my ears as Tori chases her around the hovel. I look at Hax and he laughs.

There's a sudden crack sound and I look at my feet. The floorboard below me snaps and I fall down onto the bottom floor with a thud and a scream. As I hit the floor, the wood cracked and I grunt. Ouch! Slowly standing up, I brush the dirt off my shoulder and look up from where I fell. Mrs Turnip's still screaming out there. I begin to go for the door when I hear;

"Where do you think you're going kid!"

I spin around to see Zammer standing in a hole in the wall. He says nothing else, he just sprints towards me. I jump out the way and he rams into the wall behind me. I laugh and he sneers back. I run towards him and kick him in the shin. He howls then throws a punch at me. I duck and his fist swings over my head.

"ZAMMER!" I turn around to see Hax running down the stairway.

Before I can say anything, Hax rugby tackles Zammer through the old wall, smashing it, and falling into the snow. I take my chance, I run towards Zammer and take the pills out of his pocket.

"Yes!" I say in glee.

Zammer swings his leg around and trips me over, the pills flying out of my hands.

"NO!"

The pills fly through a hole in the wall and I see Clint catch it.

"GIVE THAT BACK!" I shout.

I run towards Clint, leaving Hax to fight his cousin Zammer. I jump through the hole in the wall and look around. Where did he go?

I sprint around the hovel to see Basset smack Clint around the side of the face. Clint growls and kicks Basset in the ribs, sending him flying back into the snow.

"BASSET!" Warwick squeaks as he runs towards him.

I slide on the snow, slipping under Clint, grabbing the pills out of his hand, then standing back up. I've got them! Clint spins around then chucks a stone at me, it hits my arm, making me drop the pills as my arm goes dead.

I fall to the floor and Clint runs towards me. I trip him up and he does an accidental back flip, landing on his head in the thick snow. He grunts and I laugh a little, still unable to feel my arm. I rummage around the snow, where are the pills?

"MOOOO!"

I spin around as Mrs Turnip sprints past, Tori is running towards me, her head held low.

"NO TORI!" I shout, but it's to late, her head hits me and I flip over, landing on her back.

Tori runs around, I'm trying to get her to stop as the pills are back there.

"TORI STOP!"

Tori comes to a halt and I fly off, landing on my back in the cold powdery snow. I spring up instantly. Where are the pills? I'm around the other side of the hovel now.

"ROCCO!" I hear Fleurs scream, "HELP!"

I spin around and look up. I gasp. Zammer is holding Fleur by the scruff of her coat, hanging her out of the hole in the wall on the second floor.

"LET GO OF ME!" she screams, squirming around.

I run under her.

"STOP IT ZAMMER!" I shout up.

Zammer sneers evilly, then drops her. The blurred colours of her coat and hair fall down quickly and land in the snow with a loud scream.

"FLEUR!" I yell running to see if she is ok.

She lies there in the snow, her amber ombre hair mixed with the snow. Her eyes are shut but she hasn't completely passed out.

"Fleur! Wake up!" I say in a hurry, shaking her.

Warwick comes running from around the hovel and gasps.

"Is she ok?" he squeaks.

"Zammer chucked her out of the hovel!" I say, worried.

Warwick pushes me to the side.

"You focus on getting your Grandma's pills Rocco, I'll make sure she's ok," He squeaks.

I nod and run round the mouldy building. I try to remember where I dropped the pills. I really hope someone like Clint didn't get to it.

BANG!

I'm sent flying backwards as a mini explosion goes off. I look up to see Zammer holding a handful of dynamite cylinders in another hole on the top floor. I gasp. How did he get those?! Why did he get those?!

He chucks another at me and there's another ear-piercing bang, fire swirling in the air for a bit.

"ROCCO!"

Hax coms running through the mist and grabs me. We run away, the mini explosions following us. We lean up against the wall, Zammer can't reach us from here.

"Always hated him," Hax smiles.

I'm glad he's trying to stay positive, but I'm freaking out!

"COME BACK 'ERE YOU SCALLY-WAG!"

I look to my right to see Mrs Turnip swing her hand bag into the air, it smacks right around Dr Flibbertigibbet's head. I forgot about him!

"Quick," Hax whispers, "C'mon."

He runs through a hole in the wall and I follow. The room is darker, with less holes. We slowly walk further towards the back, it's way too quiet. BANG! There's another explosion that nearly knocks me off my feet. Splinters of wood are sent flying everywhere. I look up, Clint walks through the smoke and punches Hax around the temple. Hax stumbles backwards and I run up to Clint, delivering a punch in his stomach. He grunts and responds with kick to my left leg, the one that I sprained. I fall onto my knees, holding my leg.

"LEAVE HIM ALONE!" Hax runs up to Clint and head butts him, "AGH!"

They both stumble back, holding their heads. I take my chance and run towards Clint, punching him in the jaw. Clint falls backwards, holding his mouth. That's when I see a small cardboard container fall out his pocket. I reach out and grab it but he stamps on my arm. I let out a small yelp of pain as I roll away from him. I stand up, I've got the pills!

Clint turns to face me then begins to sprint forwards. I brace myself, thinking he's going to hit me. But instead Hax jumps on him with a loud crash.

I stare at them both fighting and a hand grabs my wrists. I turn around and see Basset standing there. He pulls me under the stair case.

"Rocco…"

He's cut off by an explosion that makes the whole hovel shake. I stare at the ruins of the wall in front of us, then turn back to him.

"Ok," he says in a rush, "I've called the police, they should get here soon, we just need to make sure no one gets hurt in the meantime."

There's another loud explosion and I look at Basset ironically.

<u>22</u>

I run out the hovel, another explosion clipping my heals. Warwick and Fleur are standing opposite Mrs Turnip in the snow.

"AAAGHHH!" Warwick yells, dashing towards Mrs Turnip and shoving her back.

I leave them to it and run to the other side of the run-down hovel. There's another loud explosion and I look up. I can see Zammer on the top floor, throwing the pieces of dynamite at the ground, he's the one who is causing the most damage.

That's when I have an idea. I run up the slope away from the hovel, gripping the pills tight in my pocket. Once I'm at the top I look around. Hmmmm, where am I going to find something I can use as a…

Sledge! My eyes are drawn to a small wooden sledge lying in some bushes. I hurry towards it. The loud explosion sounds and screams of the fight going on still ringing in my ears. I reach out, grab the sledge, then try to yank it out from the bush but the leaves and twigs pull it back. I give it one more pull and it finally comes out. Ok, now it's time to stop Zammer.

I sprint back up the slope and put the old sledge on the top. I jump on and slide down the hill at full speed. I try to aim for a lump in the snow this time. When I hit it, I go flying through the air, above all the fighting and mini explosions. I look down and see Tori jump on Clint.

The sledge soars through the air as I look around. I want to try to aim for the second floor of the hovel. I brace myself, then crash through the wall, destroying some of the remaining green wood planks.

Zammer spins around and chucks a piece of dynamite at me. I duck and it goes flying out the hole in the wall I just created, setting off when it hits the floor, causing the whole hovel to shake.

I run up to Zammer and kick him in the ribs. He doubles over, grunts, then drops the dynamite. We both look at it. I make a jump to grab it, but Zammer punches me mid jump, sending me crashing to the floor. He sneers and picks the dynamite back up.

"You really thought it would be that easy," he spits evilly.

I check my pocket, making sure the pills are still there. They are, thank goodness, but what do I do about this mad bomber?!
Zammer throws another punch at me but I duck out of the way of this one, then deliver a fist to the side of his head. He stumbles backwards and I walk towards him.

"Hand over the dynamite," I say confidently.

He sneers and chucks one at me. I dodge it and it explodes mid-air behind me, causing the floor to shake. I turn around, choking on the smoke, to see Clint walk through it. I turn back to Zammer, he jumps down out the hole in the wall.

"You can deal with the kid," he says as he disappears.

I turn back to Clint and he shoves me to the ground. The floorboards bend as I hit the floor.

"Why are you doing this Clint?" I ask, hoping that a sentimental route would be better, "I thought you and my parents were friends!"

"We were," He scorns, "but then your dad fired me from my favourite job, and out of anger, I stole a log from Hax's wheelbarrow, then chucked it at their car, causing it to tip over and kill them both. I waited in the woods, hoping to hear news about your parent's health. That's when I see Hax running through the woods with a baby in his hands. I step towards him, causing a twig to snap, thinking of asking him whether or not Cain and Sasha are ok, but I realise that it wasn't the right time."

I look at him in disgust. How dare he do that to my family!

"AAAAGGGGHHHHHHH!" I shout, running towards him and aiming a punch at him.

He ducks under my punch and grabs my shoulder. Pain seers through it as he squeezes it with all his might.

BANG!

There's another explosion beneath me. I fall through the floor, crashing to the bottom. My head aches. Through the smoke I can see blue and red flashing lights. And the sound of sirens, it reminds me of my only memory of the car crash. I see six figures running towards me, then make them out to be Hax, Tori, Fleur, Basset, Warwick and Dr Flibbertigibbet.

"Rocco!" says Hax, "are you ok?"

I hear Fleur sniff and Basset towers over me.

"Rocco, you're ok," he says with a smile.

Tori moos and I faint.

23

I wake up in Hax's arms, the police and all the others standing around me.

"Rocco!" squeaks Warwick, "He's awake everyone!"

Fleur hugs me and I slowly get up.

"What happened?" I ask.

"There was an explosion," says Dr Flibbertigibbet, "and you fell down here."

I look around, I'm in the hovel still.

"You must've hit your head hard on the way down," says Fleur.

I feel in my pocket and the pills are still there.

"Clint, Zammer and Mrs Turnip were sent to prison," says Basset with a smile, "they'll pay for what they have done by spending the rest of their lives in jail."

Tori moos with agreement as I slowly get up.

"Rocco?" says Hax, standing up with me, "are you ok?"

"I'm fine," I say with a faint smile, "but after all this, can I please give these to Grandma!"

Hax smiles.

"Yes."

"We can take you home in the police car," a policeman says, stepping forwards.

I smile.

"Thank you!"

We drive along the snowy road, it's night time. The snowy village is slightly lit up by street lamps. I look at Hax and Tori, Hax hugs me and I whisper;

"Thank you for everything," into his ear.

The police car comes to a slow stop outside Fleur's house.

"Oh, that's my stop!" Fleur says, opening the door and stepping out into the snow.

I watch her as she runs down her driveway towards her house. She stops, turns around back to us and waves.

"Bye!" her voice can be heard slightly through the car and the slowly falling snow.

Her mum opens the door and light falls onto the driveway. She runs up to Fleur and hugs her as the police drive off down the road.

We drive past the completely empty house that was once owned by Mrs Turnip, then we arrive at mine. I get out of the car, followed by Hax and Tori. Basset and Warwick went back to their 'gritting lorry company'. When I breath smoke comes out of my mouth. Hax and Tori stand next to me.

"Go on then," Hax says, pointing to the front door.

I walk up to it and knock as the police car drives off. The door is immediately opened by Grandma who bursts into tears.

"ROCCO DARLING, I WAS SO WORRIED ABOUT YOU!" she sobs.

She hugs me and I can smell her cooking on her apron. We break apart I hand her the pills. She takes them and holds them to her heart.

"Thank you," she says with a sigh, "come in! I made cookies!"

I look at Hax and Tori, smile, then walk into the warm house.